The
Pigs' Wedding

Also by Helme Heine

Friends
The Most Wonderful Egg in the World
The Pearl
One Day in Paradise

Aladdin Books
The Three Little Friends Books
The Alarm Clock
The Racing Cart
The Visitor

The Pigs' Wedding

Written and illustrated by
Helme Heine

Margaret K. McElderry Books

Porker Pig built a big fire and made smoke signals that said:
Tomorrow . . is . . Porker's . . wedding
Tomorrow . . is . . Porker's . . wedding
You . . are . . all . . invited

The pigs squealed for joy and came
from far and near to see Porker
and Curlytail, his bride, be married.
   But when they arrived on the wedding day, Curlytail whispered to
Porker, "What a lot of guests we have! And how nice they are!
But" — she sniffed — "they do smell."

Porker sniffed too. Curlytail was right. They did smell!

He called to their guests, "Friends, we're glad you have come, but you have to get cleaned up for a wedding. So come on and let me give you a bath." He picked up a hose and gave each of them a good shower.

When they were all clean, Curlytail said,
"Now we must dress them up!"

Porker had forgotten all about clothes for the wedding, but he thought quickly and came up with a brilliant idea. "Wait a minute," he said and ran off to the barn. A moment later he trotted out with a wheelbarrow full of paint pots.

"We'll paint on our party clothes," Porker said.

Each pig got just the clothes he or she had always wanted, and everything fitted perfectly. The preacher's robe was comfortable over his stomach; the bride's gown fitted like a glove. Porker gave them wrist-watches that didn't need winding, spectacles that didn't have to be cleaned, buttons that didn't pop off, and neck-ties and sashes that stayed tied. He gave himself a cigar that wouldn't go out. Everyone was happy.

Then Curlytail asked, "Porker, where is your top hat?" "Wait a minute," said Porker, because he had another good idea. He took an empty paint can, painted it black, and put it on. Now he had a splendid top hat. Next he picked some flowers, wove them into a bridal wreath, and put it on Curlytail's head.

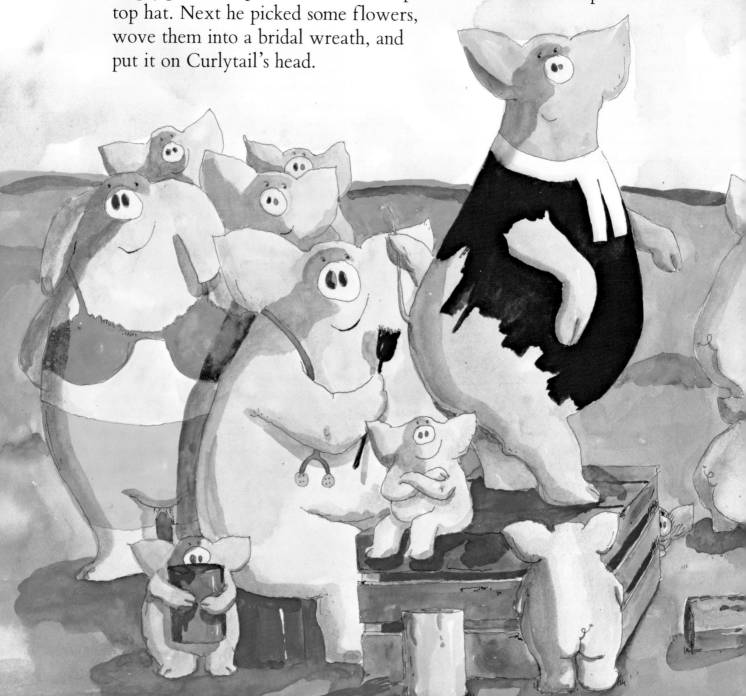

Now they were ready to have their pictures taken. The wedding party proudly lined up for the photographer who had a real camera, not a painted one, and colour film.

Curlytail and Porker were married under a huge old oak tree. Their mothers both cried, but the bride and bridegroom were so happy that they forgot about anyone else. The guests sang a song to them.

"Every piggie, small or big,
Wants to be a lucky pig!"

After the wedding ceremony the pigs ran to the table where the feast was laid out. They were hungry and thirsty from all the singing. Some of them ate and drank so much that their painted clothes burst, because their stomachs were so full. But who cared about clothes when the food tasted so good.

Then the musicians began to play. The newlyweds started the dance. They whirled and hopped across the meadow, lifting each other into the air, humming in time to the music, holding each other tight and wishing the dance would never end. The other pigs joined in, and soon they were all dancing across the meadow.

They were dancing so hard and having such a good time that they didn't notice the black clouds gathering in the sky. Suddenly the clouds burst and the wedding party was drenched with rain. They ran for shelter, but the rain was quicker than they were. It washed off all their dresses and suits, their pearl necklaces and silk ties, the spectacles, the comfortable shoes and the wrist-watches, and even Porker's fat cigar.

When the rain finally stopped, Porker shook off the raindrops and said, "Stop crying, everyone. We're wet enough already. Follow me!" He had had another brilliant idea! Running behind him, one after another, each pig took a flying leap into the mud-pond — and each, with a great SPLAT, landed right in the delicious, oozy black mud. What a *wonderful* idea it was!

That evening the newlyweds said goodbye to all their guests. After all the pigs had left, happy, muddy, and full of good food, Porker picked up Curlytail in his arms and carried her into the stable. Somewhere he had heard that was what a bridegroom should do.

In the barn, he kissed his wife gently and said, "Curlytail, I have a wonderful idea — wait a minute!" He pushed the straw aside and carefully painted on the barn wall a beautiful four-poster bed, the most beautiful bed any pig had ever seen. And, cuddled close together, they fell asleep, dreaming happy pig dreams.

Originally published as *Na warte, sagte Schwarte*
Copyright © 1977 by Gertraud Middelhauve Verlag GmbH & Co. KG Cologne
Translation copyright © 1978 by Chatto and Windus Ltd.
Margaret K. McElderry Books
An imprint of Simon & Schuster Children's Publishing Division
1230 Avenue of the Americas
New York, New York 10020
Printed in Hong Kong by South China Printing Company (1988) Ltd.
3   4   5   6   7   8   9   10
Library of Congress Cataloging-in-Publication Data
Heine, Helme.
[*Na warte, sagte Schwarte*. English]
The pigs' wedding/Helme Heine.—1st Aladdin Books ed.
p.   cm.
Translation of: *Na warte, sagte Schwarte*.
Summary: Two pigs marry and celebrate with their friends
in splendid fashion.
ISBN 6-689-50409-8
[1. Pigs—Fiction.   2. Weddings—Fiction.]   I. Title.
PZ7.H3678Pi   1991
[E]—dc20   90-40996   CIP   AC